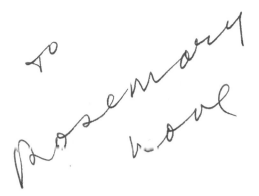

To
Rosemary
love

D0101624

One-Minute
Animal
Stories

Susan
Hewes
x

One-Minute
Animal
Stories
by
Shari Lewis
Illustrated by Kelly Oechsli

DOUBLEDAY & COMPANY, INC.
GARDEN CITY, NEW YORK

Also by Shari Lewis:

One-Minute Bedtime Stories

One-Minute Favorite Fairy Tales

Library of Congress Cataloging-in-Publication Data

Lewis, Shari.
   One-minute animal stories.

   Summary: A collection of twenty familiar and not-so-
familiar one-minute stories involving animals.
   1. Animals—Juvenile fiction. 2. Children's stories.
[1. Animals—Fiction. 2. Short stories] I. Oechsli, Kelly,
ill. II. Title.
PZ5.L6On 1986   [E]   85–16008
ISBN 0-385-19563-X

Contents

One-Minute Animal Stories

To the Parents

My book publisher husband recently commented, "Isn't it nice that now they're making books into home videos?" Knowing his inclinations in this area, I suspiciously asked, "What's so nice about it?" And he replied, "Well, a video takes less time to finish than a real book, which should leave people with more time to do the things they say they never have time to do, things like—reading!"

Well, maybe.

Frankly, I find that with the electronic diversions and distractions of television, home video, recordings, video games—and heaven knows *what's* to come next—the only way to have time for reading is by doing just that: isolating a period as "reading" time. And for so many reasons, it's doubly important to set aside time in which to read to our kids.

The latest surveys, as reported in the International Reading Association Newsletter, say, "Vocabulary is experienced by the listener long before it's comprehended by the reader. Children with 'educated' ears consistently become better reading students." The evidence is convincing: reading aloud to your youngster is the best way to create a lifelong reader.

Obviously, for reading to become a permanent part of your life, it has to be an enjoyable experience. I find that these *One-Minute Animal Stories* not only deliver pleasure, they also encapsulate powerful social messages in playful, palatable packages. However, today's kids are visibly turned off by storytellers who "sell" the good thoughts or deeds in their tales as though they were commercials, so I suggest that you just *tell* your stories, don't *sell* them. The built-in messages will sell themselves.

These animal dramas portray human life in miniature. The action between the animals parallels human conflicts, and illuminates bits of practical wisdom that have become as much a part of our culture as stories from the bible. It's astounding to realize that the morals on which these stories are based are as applicable today as they were twenty-five hundred years ago, when some of them were written.

Why are these stories of animals that talk and act like people so effective? If you've ever been passionate about a pet, you know the answer. Most of us, at one time or another, have peered into our pet's face and said, "I know you can talk. Just say something to me—anything! I promise I won't tell." And having accepted the fantasy that animals can communicate, we're able to entertain the idea that our dog or cat is observing our relationships and passing judgment on our lives, like some kind of fuzzy sage. But your child is not likely to feel pressured by the advice being offered and resent it as "teaching" or "preaching." After all, you're just reading an anecdote about animals, so it can't relate to the child who is listening, can it? But, of course, it does!

These old animal tales were probably a part of your upbringing, as they were of mine. Since we all yearn to pass on our history (so our youngsters can know what came before and learn from it), perhaps these little tales are especially also worth repeating because they create a bridge from our childhood to our child.

Tolstoy felt that children's early impressions were so important that he wrote some books for kids, and then said, "Now I can die in peace."

I think that's a bit dramatic, but I'll bet when you end the day by reading to your youngster, you'll both sleep better. Tonight, don't send your kids to bed, *put* them to bed—with a One-Minute Animal Story. I wish you sweet dreams!

Shari Lewis

Aesop's Dog

Aesop was a man who wrote fables about animals. Now one definition of fable is "a short story not founded on fact." The short story you're about to read is not a fable—it is said to be a true adventure that happened near the end of Aesop's life, twenty-five hundred years ago.

Aesop was accused of stealing a gold cup from the temple. The law said that anyone who stole from the temple was to be killed, and now the soldiers were coming to get Aesop.

Actually, he didn't do it! Nevertheless, Aesop decided to run away.

His friends knew he hadn't stolen the cup, and they were hurrying through the woods with Aesop, trying to persuade him to come back and prove he was not guilty. But Aesop said, "They intend to kill me, and so I must escape." His friends told him that no one could outrun all of the soldiers chasing him.

8

At that moment Aesop's dog took off, chasing after a rabbit. Now, in raccs with the other hounds, Aesop's dog had always been the fastest of all, so Aesop's friends said, "Hey, Aesop, your dog is sure to have rabbit for dinner tonight!"

But Aesop shook his head. "No," he said, "I'll put my money on the rabbit winning this race."

And at that moment the rabbit scurried down a rabbit hole and got away. Aesop said, "You see, my friends, the rabbit outran my dog, as I will outrun the soldiers—for it's one thing to run for your dinner, but quite another to run for your life."

The Fox
and the Ant

One day a fox boasted that he was the fastest animal in the forest, and the rabbits and squirrels didn't argue with him, because they were afraid of being eaten.

But a little ant spoke up and said, "Quit your boasting, Mr. Fox—I am faster than you are." Well, the fox only laughed, so the ant challenged him.

Now, the fox didn't want to look like a fool in front of the rest of the animals, so he stood a little in front of the ant, ready to race. The ant hopped on the fox's tail and shouted, "One, two, three—GO!"

The fox began to run. As he did, the ant climbed up the fox's tail, along his back, across his forehead and onto the tip of his nose. And when the fox arrived at the finish line, the ant hopped off his nose and shouted up from the grass, "What took you so long? I've been waiting here five minutes!"

Of course, the rabbits and squirrels knew what had happened, but that fox never did catch on!

The City Mouse and the Country Mouse

The city mouse paid a visit to his cousin, the country mouse, who lived in a tiny mouse house deep in the woods.

Country mouse served his city cousin a meal that consisted of a few leaves and some nuts. Their beds were nothing but sticks of straw in a sardine can. There was no TV. Life was really simple, and the city mouse was—well, really unimpressed.

"Come visit *me*," city mouse said. "I'll show you how life should be lived."

A week later, country mouse arrived in town.

City mouse lived in a hole in the floor of an apartment belonging to a rich man who owned two TV sets, silk drapes, thick carpets, and a cat.

"Wait until you see the fancy food I'm going to steal for our dinner," city mouse said. But as he scampered across the carpet, the cat attacked. City mouse ran for his life and barely made it back to the hole, shaking and pale. He found the country mouse packing his tiny bag.

"Goodbye," said the country cousin. "I'm going back to my home in the woods. My pleasures may be much simpler than yours, but at least I'll be alive to enjoy them!"

The Further Adventures
of Mary's Little Lamb

Mary had a little lamb, its fleece was white as snow,
And everywhere that Mary went, the lamb was sure to go.

It followed her to class one day, which was against the rule,
It made the children laugh and play, to see a lamb at school.

And so the teacher turned it out, but still it lingered near,
To wait quite patiently about, till Mary would appear.

That day, as these things happen, there was a heavy snow,
It piled up four feet off the ground,
    and on the lamb, you know.

All throughout that morning, the snow fell on and on,
And when at last the school was out,
    they thought the lamb had gone.

The teacher said, "Lambs shouldn't be in school,"
    that's what this proved,
When suddenly a "Baaaa" was heard,
    and a pile of snowflakes *moved!*

All at once, as Mary looked (and to her great surprise),
The snowdrift magically developed two enormous eyes.

It was the lamb! "Okay, the lamb can stay," the teacher
    stated,
And from that day the lamb attended school. It graduated!

The Elephant's Child

Children have always asked "Why?" questions. Some grown-ups are embarrassed when they don't know the answer to the "why" questions. Not Rudyard Kipling. If he didn't know an answer, he'd make one up. For example, when Mr. Kipling was asked, "Why do elephants have such long noses?" he replied:

There was a time when elephants didn't have long trunks. They had fat, round noses as big as beaks.

Now, the youngest elephant asked lots of questions. Her grandmother finally said, "Stop asking 'why' all the time!" So the next day, when the elephant came upon a crocodile lying in the mucky mud by the side of a stream, she asked a "what" question instead.

"Mr. Crocodile," she said, "what do you eat for supper?"

The crocodile said, "It's a secret, but if you put your head down I'll whisper it in your ear."

Baby elephants love secrets, so she did, and *snap!* the crocodile caught her by the nose and began to pull her into the water, saying, "Today for supper, I will have baby elephant!"

Well, that crocodile pulled, but the young elephant was still the stronger of the two and all the crocodile did as he pulled was to stretch the baby's nose. It became longer and longer.

At last the crocodile let go and swam away. The baby soaked her aching nose in the water to try to shrink it, but it had been stretched all out of shape. And that is why elephants have such long noses to this very day!

How the Rhinoceros Got His Saggy, Baggy Skin

Here's Mr. Kipling's answer to another "why" question:

Far away, on a deserted beach, a man took flour and water and plums and sugar and things and baked himself a huge cake.

As he was about to eat it, a rhinoceros came to the beach. Those days, the rhinoceros's skin fitted him tightly, with no wrinkles anywhere.

The rhinoceros spiked that cake on the horn of his nose and he ate it. The angry man jumped up and down and re-cited:

"Them that takes cakes
Which this baker man bakes,
Makes dreadful mistakes."

Five weeks later, during a heat wave, everybody took off all their clothes. Even the rhinoceros took off his skin and left it on the beach as he wad-dled into the water (those days, his skin buttoned underneath

with three buttons and looked like a raincoat).

That baker man smiled one smile that ran all the way around his face two times. He filled the rhinoceros's skin with all the old, dry, stale, tickly cake crumbs it could possibly hold.

When the rhinoceros came out and put on his skin again, it tickled like cake crumbs in a bed. In desperation he rubbed against a palm tree. He rubbed so hard that he rubbed his skin into a great fold over his shoulders, and another fold underneath, where the buttons used to be (he had rubbed the buttons off).

Finally he went home, very angry indeed and horribly scratchy: from that day to this, every rhinoceros has had great folds in his skin and a very bad temper, all on account of the cake crumbs inside. And do you know what? That baker man is *still* smiling!

Why Dogs Sniff Each Other's Tails

North American Indians, too, always tried to answer their children's "why" questions—sometimes with long, lovely legends, occasionally with short, sweet, silly stories like this one.

It happened one night, long ago. The dogs from all the neighboring Indian villages got together to have a dance. Even dogs from tribes that were fighting one another came to the dance, for no matter how their masters felt, the dogs did not have a bone to pick with each other.

Then, as now, some dogs had long, thin tails, others, fluffy ones. A few had tails that curved up over their backs, but most had tails that were droopy and could trip them as they danced, so it was agreed that everyone would take off his or her tail and hang it on the lowest branches of the nearby fir trees.

That's what they did, and the dancing began.

Suddenly there was a crash of thunder and a crack of lightning. Now, from living with the Indians, the dogs knew that you shouldn't remain under trees during a lightning storm, so they became frightened.

Each dog quickly snatched any old tail he or she could grab from a branch, and they scurried back to their own villages. That's why dogs always sniff each other. They want to find their own tails, once and for all!

The Dog and the Wolf

A watchdog was guarding his house one night when he heard a wolf trying to get a lid off the garbage can. The dog grabbed the wolf by the scruff of the neck, but the wolf whimpered, "Please don't hurt me—I didn't mean any harm. I was hungry and looking for something to eat." The dog said, "Yucch! Why would you want to eat the dirty stuff in the garbage can?"

The wolf explained that it wasn't always easy living in the woods. It was cold and wet and sometimes there wasn't much food out there.

The watchdog felt so sorry for the wolf, he suggested that the wolf move in with him and help keep thieves away from the house. The wolf liked that idea, and followed the dog up to the front door. By the light on the porch, the wolf suddenly saw a mark on the dog's neck.

"Oh, that's nothing," said the dog, "just the mark from the chain." "The chain!" said the wolf. "What chain?" The dog shrugged. "My master chains me up in the daytime so I won't chase after people and scare them. But I'm free every night. Believe me, it's worth it to get three good meals a day and a warm bed."

"No, thanks," said the wolf. "You can keep your three meals and other comforts. I'll take a dry crust and my freedom over a chain around my neck any day!"

The Baron
and the Bear

"I'll never forget it!" said Baron Munchausen softly. His listeners leaned forward because they knew that once he told this tall tale, they'd never forget it, either!

"I had hiked far into the woods. I was asleep at midnight when I felt something poking at me. I rolled over and found myself face to face with a great grizzly bear.

"I jumped out of my sleeping bag and ran! The bear followed, bellowing at the top of his lungs.

"I ran through woods, wallowed across streams, scampered up one hill and down another with that big beast

24

behind me, when suddenly I reached a dead end.

"On three sides of me were rock walls—on the fourth, that gigantic grizzly, galloping toward me at full speed.

"Do you know what I did then?" Baron Munchausen asked his listeners. "I stuck my hand deep inside that old grizzly's mouth. I reached all the way down and grabbed the bear's tail from the inside. I pulled on that tail and turned that beast inside out!

"Well, pulling him inside out also turned the bear around so he was facing away from me, and he was so confused that he just kept on running in the other direction!"

The Musicians of Bremen

When an old donkey's master began to wonder how much he could get for the donkey's skin, the donkey ran away.

He met a hound dog, who wailed, "I'm too old to run with the hunt, and my master has turned me out."

"You've a loud voice," said the donkey. "Come be a musician in Bremen with me."

Continuing along, they came across an old rooster and an elderly cat.

"You have strong voices too," said the donkey and the dog. "Join the troupe!"

Toward nightfall they saw a house nearby. "Maybe they'll put us up for the night, for it's cold in the woods." But when they peeked in the window, they realized they were at a robbers' den.

The animals came up with a plan. The donkey placed his front feet on the window ledge with the dog on his back. The cat climbed onto the dog's back, and the rooster clung to the cat's head.

Then each sang his own song: the donkey brayed, the dog barked, the cat mewed, and the rooster crowed. They made such an awful noise that the windowpanes splintered and crashed, and, figuring that demons had burst into the house, the robbers fled to the forest.

After that the robbers never dared go near their house again, and the four would-be Musicians of Bremen were so happy that they never left their new home. For all I know, they are there still.

Five Million Ducks

Two old-timers were arguing about which part of America had the strangest weather of all, when one of them told this tall tale:

"As a boy, I lived in Colorado. Now, if you want a place for strange weather, that's it! I remember one day I was out duck hunting when I came upon this river that was just covered with ducks. I mean, there must have been five million ducks sitting on the water.

"It had been a warm afternoon, but as the sun went down it suddenly turned so cold that the water froze, all in an instant. The ducks found their feet were stuck solidly in the ice. They got so scared that all five million ducks tried to fly away at the same time. They flapped and flapped, and the whacking of their wings raised such a wind that a whole forest of trees fell over. The sound of those trees falling got the ducks so excited that they flapped even harder, creating such an upward pull that the ice lifted away with them, and those five million ducks flew off with the entire frozen river, leaving behind nothing but a big hole that stretched for miles."

The other old-timer said, "I never heard of a hole that stretched for miles anywhere in Colorado."

"Sure you have," said the tall-tale teller. "They call it the Grand Canyon, and it's as deep as it was the day those ducks all flew away!"

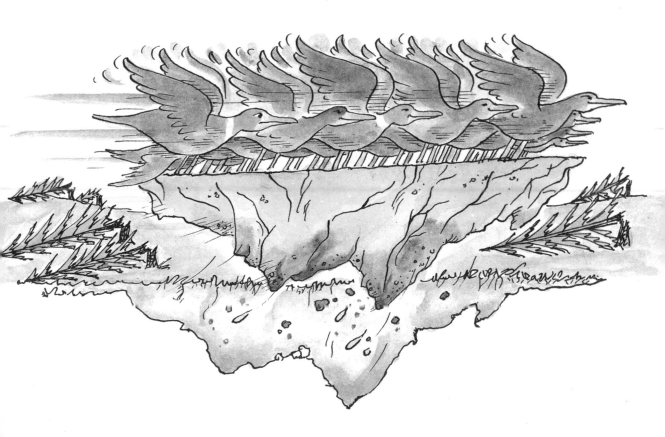

The Fox, the Crow and the Cheese

Once upon a time, a crow spied a piece of cheese on a window ledge. She decided that it would make a tasty treat, so she flew down and scooped it up in her beak. Then she flew back to her spot in the tree, ready to gobble it up.

A fox below had seen her snatch the cheese. He wanted it for himself, so he trotted to the base of the tree where the crow was perched.

"Good morning, Madam Crow," he said. "My, you look beautiful today. How shiny your feathers are, and your claws . . . why, they're just wonderful to see!" The crow was delighted with the compli-

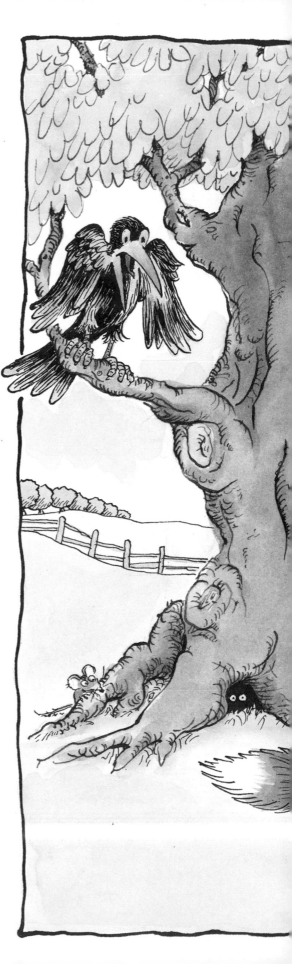

30

ments, and she wriggled all over with pleasure, so the fox continued. "Madam Crow," he said in a charming way, "I have been told that you have the loveliest voice in the forest. I would be so happy if you would sing a song for me. In fact, it would make my day!"

Well, the crow had never heard her voice praised (for as you know, crows make awful sounds) and she was so flattered that she opened her beak to sing to him, to give him the pleasure he seemed to crave. But the moment she did so, the cheese fell from her beak and into the waiting jaws of the fox, who ate it all up!

Goldilocks

Walking through thc woods onc day, Goldilocks found a house.
It was too small for a giant, it was too big for a mouse.

She saw three chairs when she walked in,
    and to her great surprise,
She found three bowls of cereal, each of a different size.

She ate the small bowl standing up, and then she saw a chair
Which she broke, of course, when she sat down . . .
    it belonged to Baby Bear.

By this time she was sleepy, so she stretched out on a bed,
The smallest, though there were two larger beds to use
    instead.

She'd been asleep for just an hour,
    when in walked three brown bears.
Their noses twitchin', they went to the kitchen,
    and saw the broken chair.

The little bear said, "Look at that, Pa, look at my little bowl.
A thief's been here, I think that's clear
    —my cereal's been stole!"

"Stolen, son," his papa said, correcting the little bear.
Then he rushed upstairs and found the girl
    named Goldilocks sleeping there.

"What do you think you're doing here?"
    Big Bear said with a shout.
Then, picking her up, bed and all, he swiftly threw her out!

Peter and the Wolf

This story should be called Peter and the Wolf and the Grandfather and the Cat and the Bird and the Duck and the Hunters, for they all have starring roles in the drama.

The Grandfather locks Peter behind a tall wall, so Peter can't get out of the garden and into trouble.

The Wolf catches the Duck and wolfs her down. The Wolf also knows a good recipe for a Bird-and-Cat casserole and the Bird and the Cat are really up a tree. I mean, really!

Peter climbs to the top of the tall wall. Under a nearby tree he sees the Wolf circling, trying to figure out how to get to the Cat and the Bird. A branch of the tree stretches over the wall, and Peter climbs onto the branch. He whispers to the Bird, "Buzz down and

keep the Wolf busy." The Bird whizzes by the Wolf's ear and tweaks his tail and the Wolf snaps and snarls. While the Wolf is thinking of nothing but getting rid of that bird brain, *permanently,* Peter drops a loop of rope around the Wolf's tail and pulls with all his might.

The Wolf is now dangling from the tree, and, hanging upside down, he coughs up the Duck, who waddles away, happy to be out of this story.

The Hunters (who know the Wolf from another fairy tale) see the Wolf and say, "Let's take him to the zoo," because wolves are an endangered species. Especially in fairy tales.

And that's the story of Peter and the Wolf and the Grandfather and the Cat and the Bird and the Hunters. The End.

Thieves Go Free

There was once a ruler who had an unusual way of punishing criminals. He would jail all of the people who bought stolen goods, but the thieves he would let go free.

"How ridiculous," his subjects complained, "to let the thieves go, when *they* are the real criminals."

One day the ruler brought his people together in front of the palace. Then he let loose a number of rabbits, and he spread some lettuce leaves on the ground. The rabbits quickly took the leaves in their mouths and scampered down their holes.

Once again, the next day, the ruler assembled everyone before his palace. He released the rabbits, and scattered lettuce leaves as he had the day before—only this time all of the rabbit holes were blocked with stones.

Once again, the rabbits took the leaves and scampered to their holes. But finding their holes blocked, they dropped the lettuce and scurried away.

Turning to his people, the ruler said, "There, you see? Thieves are not as guilty as those to whom they sell their loot. If no one would buy the stuff, the thieves would give up stealing immediately. That's why I punish the people who buy stolen goods, and in my kingdom, thieves go free!"

The Baron and the Buck

"One time, I went deer hunting," Baron Munchausen began. "It was a long, cold winter and a lot of hungry people were counting on me to bring home this big buck. I'd been trailing the animal for days, and the only thing left to eat in my backpack was a bag of cherries.

"On this morning, I was following the beast's hoofprints. Suddenly I heard a noise. I whipped around, and there was that deer, not two hundred feet away. He had little stumps instead

38

of big horns—his antlers had probably been broken off in a fight with another big buck.

"I grabbed my rifle, and then, with a groan, I remembered that I had left the bullets in the cookie jar back home—but that didn't stop me. I popped a dozen cherries into my mouth, spit the pits into my hand, loaded those pits into the barrel of the gun, and fired right between the eyes. The deer ran off, so I figured I had missed.

"Next spring, I went back to those same woods and I came across that very same deer. I knew it was the deer that I had shot the winter before, because right between his eyes, where his antlers should have been, this deer had grown—*a cherry tree!*"

Peter Rabbit

Once upon a time, there were four little rabbits. Their names were Flopsy, Mopsy, Cottontail and Peter. They had only one suit of clothes amongst them, and on Tuesday it was Peter's turn to wear those clothes.

Mrs. Rabbit said he could pick berries in the lane, but the one place he mustn't go was Farmer McGregor's garden. So, of course, that was the one place that Peter went. After eating enough cabbage to develop a fat tummy, who did Peter run into but Farmer McGregor himself!

"Stop, thief!" cried the farmer (who had no use for rabbits), and he began to chase Peter. Peter was frightened, and he scrambled this way and that. He lost one of his shoes amongst the carrots and the other amongst the potatoes. He tore the buttons off his jacket on a wire fence, and then he jumped into a bucket to hide—only to find it full of water. As he hid shivering in the water, his jacket shrank. When he tried to hop to safety, his fat little belly got him stuck between the slats of a fence, and he barely got away from the angry Mr. McGregor. But Peter *did* manage to get home.

By the time he raced through the door, he had a cold in his nose, and he didn't have a stitch of clothes on his body, so from that day on, Flopsy, Mopsy, Cottontail and Peter had nothing to wear. But I think rabbits look better like that anyway, don't you?

The Donkey's Shadow

To travel across the desert, a man once hired an Arab's donkey, strapped his bags to the donkey's back, climbed aboard and rode off, with the Arab poking the animal from behind.

After a while the hot, tired traveler got off the donkey's back and went to sleep in the animal's tiny shadow.

Soon the Arab, who also found the heat unbearable, took the reins of the donkey and pulled him forward a few feet. Naturally the donkey's shadow moved with the animal, and in that shadow the Arab lay down.

The traveler was angry to awaken and find himself in the sun.

The Arab said, "The donkey is mine and so is his shadow."

"I have hired the donkey, and therefore I have hired his shadow as well," said the traveler. They began to fight.

The donkey became frightened and ran away, leaving the silly fellows with neither donkey nor shadow. Which proves that if you fight over the shadow, you may lose the real thing.

The Bat

They say that once, an army of animals was about to advance against an army of birds. A curious winged creature flew amongst the animals.

They asked, "Are you a bird or a beast?"

"People call me a bat," he said. "But I am surely an animal. I have fur all over my body."

So the animals invited him to fight with them against the birds. But when the birds began winning, the bat flew into a low cloud and came out where the birds were circling.

"Who are you?" the birds asked.

"People call me a bat," he said, "but I'm certainly a bird. Look at my wings."

Well, they invited him to fight with *them* against the animals, and so the battle went on.

The animals did better one day and the birds, the next. And each time the tide turned, the bat turned as well—first he fought with the birds, then, as they seemed to be losing, with the animals.

The battle ended with neither winners nor losers. Everyone was happy, except the bat.

The birds wanted nothing to do with him, nor did the animals. Because he only wanted to be on the winning side, he ended up on none.

And to this day, the bat seems to be doomed to hang upside down, in dark caves or on out-of-the-way trees— shunned by all.

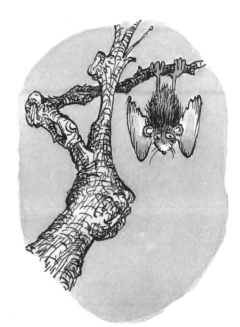

45

The Monkey and the Cheese

Two cats had stolen a piece of cheese. They agreed to divide it in half, but were arguing about its size.

"It's eight inches long," said the Siamese cat.

"Seven," purred the Persian.

A monkey, who was a friend to both cats, said he'd be the judge so his friends wouldn't fight.

The monkey held the cheese in his paws. "Trouble is," he said, "it's an uneven shape." He bit one side of the cheese and handed it back to the cats.

"Now it's five inches long," snarled the Siamese.

"Four," pouted the Persian.

So the monkey took another bite. "What do you think now, friends?" he asked.

The Siamese snapped, "About an inch long."

"Half inch," the Persian persisted.

The monkey needed both hands free to separate his fighting feline friends, so he popped the rest of the cheese into his mouth and swallowed it.

"I've tried to help you," the monkey said, as he pulled the cats apart. "I only wish I had been able to satisfy *you* as much as I've satisfied me."

And he left—quickly!

World-famous ventriloquist, puppeteer, and author of twenty-seven books, **Shari Lewis** has been honored with five Emmy Awards, a Peabody, the Monte Carlo TV Award for World's Best Variety Show, and the 1983 Kennedy Center Award for Excellence and Creativity in the Arts. One of a select few female symphony conductors, she has led more than 100 symphony orchestras throughout the United States and Canada, including the National Symphony at Kennedy Center, the Pittsburgh Symphony, and the National Arts Centre Orchestra of Canada.

Shari Lewis is author of the recently published *One-Minute Favorite Fairy Tales*. Her previous book for Doubleday, *One-Minute Bedtime Stories,* is a juvenile bestseller and has been made into home videos by Worldvision Enterprises. Also available is "The Shari Lewis Home Entertainment Library," by MGM/UA, which includes three hour-long cassettes: *Have I Got a Story for You!, You Can Do It,* and *Kooky Classics.* Shari Lewis is presently Chairman of the Board of Trustees of the International Reading Foundation and has served on the National Board of the Girl Scouts of the U.S.A. A resident of Beverly Hills, California, Ms. Lewis is married to book publisher Jeremy Tarcher; their daughter, Mallory, recently graduated from Columbia University and is Eastern Regional Marketing Director of New World Pictures, home video division.

Kelly Oechsli has illustrated over seventy books for children. Born in Butte, Montana, he received his training at the Cornish School of Art in Seattle, Washington. An Army ski instructor in World War II, he now divides his recreation time between tennis and gardening.